LITTLE SIMON

An imprint of Simon & Schuster Children's Publishing Division • 1230 Avenue of the Americas, New York, New York 10020 • First Little Simon hardcover edition March 2017 • Copyright © 2017 by Simon & Schuster, Inc. All rights reserved, including the right of reproduction in whole or in part in any form. LITTLE SIMON is a registered trademark of Simon & Schuster, Inc., and associated colophon is a trademark of Simon & Schuster, Inc. For information about special discounts for bulk purchases, please contact Simon & Schuster Special Sales at 1-866-506-1949 or business@simonandschuster.com. The Simon & Schuster Speakers Bureau can bring authors to your live event. For more information or to book an event contact the Simon & Schuster Speakers Bureau at 1-866-248-3049 or visit our website at www.simonspeakers.com. Series designed by Laura Roode. Book designed by Hannah Frece. The text of this book was set in Usherwood.

Manufactured in the United States of America 0217 FFG

10 9 8 7 6 5 4 3 2 1

Cataloging-in-Publication Data is available from the Library of Congress.

ISBN 978-1-4814-8590-6 (hc)

ISBN 978-1-4814-8589-0 (pbk)

ISBN 978-1-4814-8591-3 (eBook)

the adventures of
SOPHIE MOUSE

10

It's Raining, It's Pouring

By Poppy Green • Illustrated by Jennifer A. Bell

LITTLE SIMON
New York London Toronto Sydney New Delhi

CONTENTS

Chapter 1

Rain, Rain, Go Away

Sophie Mouse ran to the window. She glanced up at the sky. The clouds looked darker than the last time she'd checked. Sophie stretched her hand outside. No raindrops.

"It's not raining yet!" Sophie cried, running back into the kitchen. Her whiskers were tingling. She could tell the rain was coming. But maybe

there was just enough time for their
picnic.

It was Sunday morning. In the
Mouse family's house at the base of

the oak tree, Mrs. Mouse had made
her famous vanilla-bean scones. As
they cooled, the sweet scent of the
vanilla filled the kitchen.

Mr. Mouse flipped huckleberry pancakes on the griddle. *Sizzle!*

Sophie and her little brother, Winston, peeked into the oven. They had worked together to make a banana-dandelion bread. It was rising! Soon it would be done!

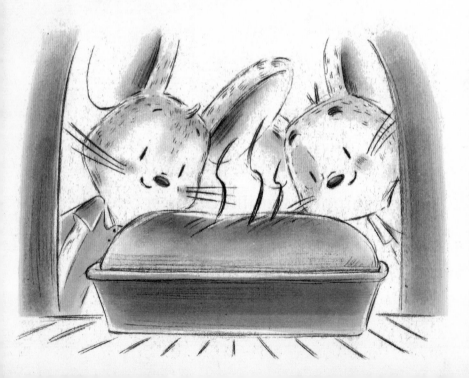

Sophie got the picnic
basket ready.
Then she ran
upstairs to the
linen closet to
get the picnic
blanket. She
had the perfect
spot in mind: on the bank of
the stream near the playground.
Afterward, she could scurry over to
Hattie's house to say hello!

Lily Mouse tucked the scones into
the basket. George Mouse added the
pancakes.

Soon the banana-dandelion bread was done and packed, along with jams and jars of mint tea.

"Okay! Let's go!" Sophie exclaimed. She picked up the basket. Winston grabbed the blanket. And the Mouse family stepped outside.

Plip! Plop! Plip!

Sophie felt three big raindrops—
one on her ear, one on her shoulder,
and one on the tip of her nose.

"Oh no!" Winston moaned.

The four mice gazed upward,
holding their palms out.

Plip! Plop! Plip! Plippity-plippity,
plop-plop-plop . . .

The rain was picking up. Winston
threw the blanket over the basket to
protect it.

"I hate to say it," said Mr. Mouse, "but I think we'd better make it an indoor picnic."

"Or," Sophie said, "it *could* be fun to have a picnic in the rain. . . ."

She smiled hophefully. But no one else seemed excited about the idea.

So back inside they went. In the living room, they pushed back the furniture and spread the blanket on the floor.

The yummy food cheered Sophie
up. But now and then, she gazed out
the window at the gray mist.

Mr. Mouse patted her on the back.
"I know it's disappointing, Sophie,"
he said. "But we could really use the

rain. We could use a lot *more* rain. It's been very dry this season."

Sophie's shoulders drooped. She took another bite of scone. She knew her dad was right, but she still couldn't help wishing the rain away.

~ Chapter 2 ~

The Project

The next morning, a ray of sunlight fell across Sophie's face.

She opened her eyes and squinted toward the window.

It figures, thought Sophie. *On a school day it's sunny out.*

It had drizzled all Sunday afternoon. Not enough rain to make puddles to play in. Just enough rain to ruin their picnic.

Sophie had spent the day painting.

As she got dressed for school, Sophie studied the three paintings drying on her easels. They were views out of different windows in their house.

Sophie laughed. She had used up most of her gray paint!

After breakfast, Sophie and Winston walked together to Silverlake Elementary. Mrs. Wise opened the door and called out, "Good morning, everyone!" just as Sophie and Winston arrived.

They went in behind Hattie Frog,

her sister Lydie, and Ellie the squirrel. They all took their seats.

Ben and James, the rabbit brothers, arrived a few moments later. Malcolm the mole and Willy the toad walked

in next. And Zoe the bluebird and Piper the hummingbird flew in too. Finally Owen Snake arrived.

"Good! Everyone is here!" said Mrs. Wise. "Because I want all of

you to hear about the unit we are starting today on . . . water."

Ugh! thought Sophie. *Hadn't they had enough water this weekend?*

Mrs. Wise went on. She explained they'd be studying the different phases of water, like ice and steam. They would learn about the water cycle. They would discuss how important water is to life.

"But first, we'll be exploring why things sink or float in water," Mrs. Wise said. "We'll even do some experiments."

Sophie perked up. Experiments? That sounded fun!

"There is also a unit project," Mrs. Wise said. "Each of you will be building a model boat."

Sophie smiled. She heard excited whispers all around the classroom. She also noticed Winston bouncing with glee in the front row. Sophie giggled. This project was *perfect* for him.

Mrs. Wise said she'd cover information in

class that would help them design a proper boat. It would be up to them to work on building the boats at home. Then, in two weeks, they'd go over to the nearby pond to test them out!

Water had just gotten a whole lot more fun!

— Chapter 3 —

Shipshape

Winston hadn't stopped talking about boat ideas since they'd left school.

"I wonder what's the best material to use," he was saying as he and Sophie walked home. "Wood, I guess. But there are so many different kinds. There's oak and ash and cedar and cypress and elm and pine and fir and—"

"Winston!" Sophie interrupted with
a laugh. "You have two whole weeks
to figure it out."

Winston hopped with excitement.
"I know! But I want to start designing

my boat *right away*!" He waved his
arms as if drawing his blueprints in
the air. "It's not going to be a model
boat. I want to build a real one. One
that could carry me!"

Sophie laughed again. "Those are big plans for a little mouse," she said.

But then Sophie remembered the amazing fort Winston had once built in the woods. He *was* great at building things, just like their dad, who was an architect.

The big oak tree came into view, their house nestled between the roots. Sophie followed Winston up the front walk, crunching an acorn cap under her foot.

Sophie stopped and looked down. She picked up an acorn cap and studied it.

Acorn caps float, thought Sophie. *Don't they?*

Sophie picked up a few more acorn caps. She carried them inside. She ran to

While Winston went on about his big plans, Sophie was lost in thought about her smaller plans. She wanted to make a tiny boat. Tiny but tough.

What floats naturally? Sophie asked herself. *Leaves float sometimes. Lily pads float. But those don't seem very sturdy. Twigs? Hattie and Owen made me that raft out of twigs.*

Sophie and Winston rounded a bend.

the bathroom and filled the tub with
water.

Then Sophie placed the acorn

caps pointy-side-down on the water's surface.

All three of them floated—like three tiny boats. Sophie added some more water to test their stability. They rocked with the waves of water, but did not sink!

Sophie smiled. She tapped her chin as she thought.

How could she build a boat that floated like an acorn cap?

— Chapter 4 —

whatever Floats your Boat

The next morning Mrs. Wise took the class down to the pond.

"This is where we will test our boats next week," she told them. "But today, we will learn more about why some objects float." She tossed a blade of grass into the pond. It floated on the water's surface. "And why other objects sink," she added.

She picked up a stone and tossed it in. *Plunk!* It sank.

"The clay soil here at this pond is perfect for our experiments," Mrs. Wise explained. "Watch!"

She scooped up a hunk of clay. "It's

crumbly since it's been so dry. But just add a little water to it."

Mrs. Wise wet the soil with pond water. Then she rolled it into a ball. She placed it on the surface of the water. It sank right away.

Then Mrs. Wise
scooped up more
clay. She wet it
and squished it
into a pancake.
She pinched up the sides to
make a bowl shape.
She flattened the
bottom. Now it
sort of looked
like a boat.

"Will this
sink?" Mrs.
Wise asked the
class. "Or float?"

Winston raised his hand to answer. "Float!" he said.

"Yes! Float!" Hattie echoed.

Most of the students agreed. Only James and Piper thought it would sink.

Mrs. Wise placed the boat on the water and let go. It was floating!

James and Piper looked confused. "But it's still made of clay," James said.

"The clay ball sank. So why not this?"

"Great question," said Mrs. Wise.

She explained how important the shape of an object was to its buoyancy—or ability to float. "Any object placed in the pond pushes some water out of the way. But the water also pushes back. It's that force that holds the object up in the water."

Mrs. Wise picked up the clay boat.

"This boat pushes a lot of water out of the way," she went on. "The ball pushed much *less* water out of the way."

Sophie thought she understood. "So an object that pushes more water out of the way has more force holding it up?" Sophie said.

Mrs. Wise beamed. "That's

correct!" she exclaimed.

The students spent the morning making different shapes out of the clay. Then they tried to float them in the pond.

Some worked very well.
Others didn't float at all.

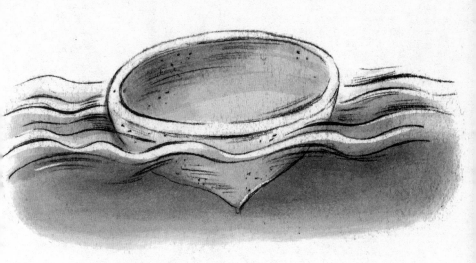

Sophie sculpted some clay into the shape of an acorn cap. When she was ready to test it, she laid it gently atop the water. It floated!

But then Willy stepped into the water, eager to test his own clay boat. He didn't see Sophie's. His foot came down right on top of it.

Sophie's boat was now sunk *and* smushed.

"Oops," said Willy sheepishly. "Sorry, Sophie."

"That's okay," Sophie said. She

fished her clay blob out of the water.
She studied the drippy mess. *Guess
that's why they don't make real
boats out of clay*, she thought.

— Chapter 5 —

In Search of Butterfly Brook

Within a couple of days, Winston had a boat blueprint drawn up. He was ready to start building. Now he needed to get his materials.

In school Mrs. Wise had explained why wood was a good choice. "Most woods are less dense than water," she had said. "So they tend to float."

Winston was way ahead of that.

At dinner each night, he peppered Mr. Mouse with questions about different woods.

"Ash is strong for its weight," Mr. Mouse had said. "And cedar doesn't rot easily."

After days of thinking it over, Winston had made a decision. At breakfast on Saturday morning, he suddenly called out: "Fir!"

Sophie looked at him, confused. "Huh?" she said.

"Douglas fir!" Winston replied. "That's the wood for my boat. It's strong, it bends without breaking, and it won't rot easily. What do you think, Sophie?"

Sophie smiled. "Sounds good to me, Winston," she said.

"There are lots of fir trees by Butterfly Brook," Mr. Mouse told them. "That might be a good place to look."

Butterfly Brook! *Yes!* thought Sophie. An excuse to go to one of her favorite places. It was home to so many different types of butter-flies. Sophie remembered the ever-green trees growing on both sides of the brook. Now she knew what kind they were.

Sophie grabbed her satchel. She

packed two water canteens—one for her and one for Winston. It had been hot and dry all week long. They needed to be prepared!

Then Sophie and Winston set off. Instead of heading toward town, they took a path going the opposite way through deeper woods.

The path twisted this way and that, around boulders and through brambles. They scrambled over lots of fallen branches and climbed up a rise.

"I'm hot," Winston said. "Can we take a water break?"

It really *was* hot out. Sophie's whiskers were wilting and water sounded good to her, too. They stopped for a minute to gulp down some water. Then they kept going.

"The brook is just up ahead," Sophie said to Winston.

They came around a bunch of ferns. Sophie stopped in her tracks. Winston stopped next to her.

Sophie looked around, confused. "That's weird," she said. "I thought Butterfly Brook would be right here."

There was a small ravine where the brook should have been. Sophie went up to the edge and looked down into it. There were some puddles at the bottom. But that was it.

"Wait," Sophie said. "This *is* the brook."

"But . . . where's the rest of the water?" Winston asked.

Sophie gasped. "It must have dried up!"

— Chapter 6 —

Trading in a Wish

Staring at the dried-up brook, Sophie remembered the crumbly clay soil at the pond. She remembered her dad saying they really needed more rain.

That was the day it rained and I wished it would stop, Sophie thought. *It hasn't rained since!*

Now Sophie felt badly about her wish.

This wasn't good. Not good at all.

Suddenly, high overhead, they heard a sharp *CRACK!* Sophie and Winston looked up.

Then came *CR-R-R-ACK!*

A branch had snapped. It was falling down—fast!

Sophie grabbed Winston's arm. She pulled him to one side.

Fwomp! The large fir branch hit the ground where Winston had been standing.

Winston looked up at Sophie. "Wow. Thanks!" he said.

"No problem," Sophie replied. "That was close."

Sophie looked around, noticing more branches on the ground. "The trees are so dry," Sophie said.

"That must be why they're dropping branches."

It was easy enough to find two large pieces of fir to take with them. Sophie and Winston each dragged a

big branch home. It would be enough
wood for both of their boats.

That evening, as they sat down to
dinner, Sophie told Mr. and Mrs.

Mouse what they had seen.

Mrs. Mouse nodded grimly. "I've never seen Pine Needle Grove so desperate for rain," she said. "The well near the bakery has dried up. I need to walk halfway to Goldmoss

Pond to get water. And that well is low too."

Mr. Mouse also looked concerned. "I ran into Malcolm Mole's parents the other day," he said. "They're farmers, you know. They say the early lettuce and peas aren't growing very well."

Mrs. Mouse sighed. "And if plants don't get enough water now, there may not be many berries in the autumn.

Then there may not be enough to can for the winter."

Before she started eating, Sophie made a silent wish for rain. She hoped it would cancel out the wish she'd made the week before.

All week long, Sophie and Winston worked on their projects after school.

Thursday was the big day! They would bring in their boats and take another field trip to the pond.

Winston was going ahead with his plan to build a full-size boat. He spent every spare minute in the backyard. There, he had set up a work area. Mr. Mouse was letting him borrow some tools. Winston was even learning to bend wood using steam!

Sophie still wasn't sure how to build her acorn-cap boat.

She tried carving a block of fir into the right shape. On Monday, she sat whittling the wood for hours. In

the end, she couldn't get the balance right. It kept tipping, filling with water, and sinking.

On Tuesday, she tried nailing wood pieces into an acorn-cap shape.

But there were too many seams and corners, even after sanding everything down.

On Wednesday afternoon, Sophie
sat staring at the three acorn caps
that had inspired her. She had to
come up with *something!*

What else can I use? Sophie asked herself. *What is shaped like an acorn cap? What's smooth like an acorn cap? What weighs about the same as an acorn cap?*

Sophie jumped up. "An acorn cap!" she cried out loud. "I can build my boat out of an actual acorn cap!"

Sophie couldn't believe she hadn't thought of it sooner!

— Chapter 7 —

Bad Surprise, Good Surprise

Sophie was a dozen steps ahead of Winston on the path to school. She stopped and waited for him for the millionth time.

Winston was pulling a wagon. Balanced on top was his finished boat.

Sophie had to admit: it was beautiful.

The boat had a cloth sail, a rudder for steering, and a built-in seat for the captain. Winston had even found time to paint it! Sophie had made a huge batch of poppy-red paint for him.

She couldn't wait to see the look on everyone's faces when they saw Winston's full-size boat!

Sophie also wanted to show off her own. She was proud of her acorn-cap boat. It was so small, especially

compared to Winston's. But it was strong and sturdy. Sophie had added a leaf sail and painted it with all sorts of bright colors and designs.

Sophie and Winston arrived at the schoolhouse a little bit late. Winston parked his boat outside. Then they hurried up the front steps.

"Good morning," Mrs. Wise greeted them. "Boats can go on the back table. Then please take your seats."

Sophie placed her boat on the table. She paused a moment to look at all the others already sitting there.

Each one was completely unique.

Sophie hurried to her desk.

"Now, class," Mrs. Wise was saying, "I can see you've all worked very hard on your boats. And I'm sure you're excited to test them in

the pond. But I'm afraid I have bad news."

The students groaned. Mrs. Wise waited for them to quiet down. Then she went on.

"I walked by the pond on the way to school. The water is almost completely dried up."

Oh no! thought Sophie. *First Butterfly Brook, and now this!*

"I'm very sorry," Mrs. Wise told them. "We'll have to wait for it to rain. Then we can reschedule our boat test."

Sophie had an uneasy feeling. She *was* disappointed that their plans were ruined. But it was more than that. She was really starting to worry about there not being any rain. Sophie had heard about

droughts. The word made her think
of deserts she had read about in
books.

Was Silverlake Forest having a
drought?

The classroom was abuzz with
questions for Mrs. Wise.

"When do *you* think it will rain

again, Mrs. Wise?" Zoe asked.

"What if it doesn't?" Ellie asked with a gasp.

"Could *all* the lakes and ponds dry up?" Willy asked. "Even Forget-Me-Not Lake?"

Mrs. Wise held up her wing. "Now, now," she said calmly. "Please, everyone. Let's not panic. Take a deep breath."

The class went silent. Mrs. Wise smiled, opened her mouth to speak, and—

BOOOOM!

A loud, sudden clap of thunder shook the schoolhouse.

Everyone jumped—even Mrs. Wise.

A second later, all the students were at the window. They looked up at the sky. Dark storm clouds were rolling in!

Sophie felt a telltale tingle in her whiskers.

"Rain!" she cried. "It's going to rain! I can feel it!"

— Chapter 8 —

when it Rains, it Pours

The next day Sophie, Hattie, and Owen sang as the whole class marched to the pond.

It's raining, it's pouring,

The old bear is snoring.

She went to bed and bumped her head,

And she couldn't get up in the morning.

It wasn't raining anymore, but it had *poured* all night. And now the boat test was back on!

The animals were singing and splashing in huge puddles the whole way to the pond. No one seemed to mind that they were getting muddy!

But Winston *was* having an extra hard time pulling his boat wagon along the muddy path. Ben and Ellie pitched in to help him pull.

"Your boat is amazing!" cried Ben.
"It's big enough to hold one of us!"
"It *is* going to hold one of us,"
Winston replied.
"Me!"

"Really?" said
Ellie. "Cool!"

Up ahead, Mrs. Wise stopped. "Look, class!" she announced, gesturing at the pond. "We have an actual pond again."

The students cheered.

"Can we put our boats in?" Winston asked.

Mrs. Wise smiled and nodded.

The students cheered and hurried down to the water's edge. Within seconds, there was a whole fleet of model boats in the water.

It took Winston a little longer to get his boat off the wagon and into the water. But soon enough he was aboard, raising the mast and getting ready to hoist the sail.

All the model boats seemed to be floating pretty well. Zoe's boat was maybe sitting a little low in the water. And Malcolm kept having to

reattach his boat's keel. But none of them had sunk!

"Hey, everybody!" called a voice from offshore. "Out here!"

Sophie looked up. It was Winston, waving from his boat. He was sailing along at a speedy clip.

Everyone waved back excitedly.

"Go, Winston!" Sophie cheered, jumping up and down.

Then suddenly, Sophie froze.

A huge rock had come loose from the slippery mud and was rolling into the water on the far side of the pond. And a huge rock meant . . . a huge wave.

Sophie's mouth fell open as the rock splashed into the water and a wave began to rise. The wave was rolling across the pond and picking up speed.

Winston didn't see it. He was sailing with his back to the wave. But it was gaining on him. And fast!

"Winston!" Sophie called out at the top of her lungs. "Look out!"

Chapter 9

Sophie's Plan

The wave swept up everything in its path—all the model boats and Winston's boat too! Winston rose up, up, up and was carried along on the crest.

Winston's boat was *surfing* the wave!

Sophie saw him look around in panic, wondering what was happening. He clutched the mast so he wouldn't fall overboard.

"Mrs. Wise!" Sophie cried. "What do we do?!"

But everything was happening so fast. All they could do was watch, unable to help. The wave carried Winston's boat right into a tangle of driftwood. The boat got snagged and the wave rolled on without it.

"Winston!" Mrs. Wise called. "Are you okay?"

"Yes!" Winston called back. "But I'm not sure my boat is!"

The sail was ripped. The mast had snapped in half.

Winston was stranded out in the middle of the pond.

"Don't worry," Mrs. Wise called.
"I'll fly over there and get you. You
can ride on my back." She spread
her powerful wings.

"Wait!" Sophie cried. "I have a
hunch Winston won't want to leave
his boat behind."

Sophie looked around and spotted some cattails.

Would one be long enough to reach Winston? Maybe one wouldn't, but a *bunch* would.

Sophie began plucking them and tying the ends together to form a long rope. Then she tied a loop at one end of the rope.

She handed it to Mrs. Wise.

"Could you fly this end over to Winston?" Sophie asked. "Then the rest of us can hold the other end and pull his boat back to shore."

Mrs. Wise nodded. She clutched the loop in her beak. Then she took off. With three mighty flaps of her wings, Mrs. Wise covered the distance to Winston. She circled overhead, dropped the loop, and lassoed Winston's broken mast. Then she fluttered down so Winston could climb onto her back.

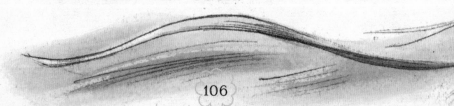

"She did it!" Sophie called out
to her classmates. "Now let's pull!
Slowly! So the rope doesn't snap."

The whole class lined up behind

Sophie to help. They pulled together
like a tug-of-war team. Slowly, inch
by inch, Winston's boat crept closer
to shore.

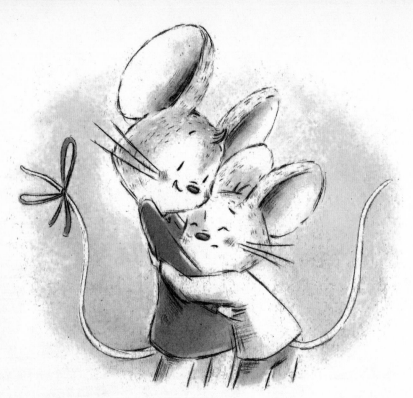

Finally, it hit land. At the same
time, Winston hopped off Mrs. Wise's
back. He ran over and hugged Sophie.

Sophie patted Winston on the back
as she hugged him. "Good thing you
built such a sturdy boat, Winston!"

Winston pulled away. He looked his boat over and frowned. "It needs some repairs," he said. Then his face brightened. "But I'll fix it up as good as new!"

Sophie laughed. "I know you will!"
she said.

In the end, the class was able to find
every one of the model boats. They

had washed up on the far side of the pond.

Some of them were a little banged up, but all of them were still afloat!

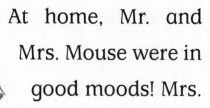

At home, Mr. and Mrs. Mouse were in good moods! Mrs. Mouse reported that the well near the bakery was nearly full again. Then she described the scene in the village when it began to rain.

"Everyone came outside and started dancing in the puddles!" Mrs. Mouse said with a laugh. "Mr. Handy of Handy's Hardware was waltzing with Ms. Reeve, the librarian."

Mr. Mouse laughed too. "Everyone is so relieved," he said. "A few more rainy days like this and we'll be just about back to normal."

Up in her room, Sophie found a special spot for her acorn-cap boat. She placed it in the corner near her easel.

Then Sophie got out a blank
canvas. She mixed up some paints.
And she began to paint a scene from
her day. She painted a mouse on a
boat surfing an enormous wave.

The painting called for a lot
of gray. And Sophie did not mind
one bit.

The End

Here's a peek at the next
Adventures of Sophie Mouse book!

Mrs. Wise flung the school door open
wide. Standing there was a well-
dressed squirrel. Sophie blinked. It
was Ellie's father. And he was holding
a big plate of cupcakes!

"Happy birthday, Ellie!" Mr. Squirrel
called out to his daughter.

Ellie hurried over to her dad and
gave him a quick hug. "Thanks for

bringing them in, Dad!" Ellie said. Then she turned to the class. "Surprise, everybody! Mrs. Wise said I could bring in a birthday treat!"

Sophie and the other students cheered.

Ellie walked around, placing a card on each student's desk.

Sophie glanced down. It was an invitation!

"Sunday is my actual birthday," Ellie explained. "I hope all of you can come to my party."

Sophie wiggled happily in her seat.

Forget the math quiz, she told herself. *It's party time!*

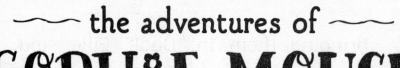

the adventures of
SOPHIE MOUSE

For excerpts, activities, and more about
these adorable tales & tails, visit
AdventuresofSophieMouse.com!